THE STATIC OF THE SPHERES

The Personal History, Adventures, Experiences & Observations of Peter Leroy, a Voluminous Fiction by Eric Kraft

Little Follies

My Mother Takes a Tumble

Do Clams Bite?

Life on the Bolotomy

The Static of the Spheres

The Fox and the Clam

The Girl with the White Fur Muff

Take the Long Way Home

Call Me Larry

The Young Tars

Herb 'n' Lorna

Reservations Recommended

Where Do You Stop?

What a Piece of Work I Am

At Home with the Glynns

Leaving Small's Hotel

Inflating a Dog

Passionate Spectator

Flying

THE STATIC OF THE SPHERES

ERIC KRAFT

THE BABBINGTON PRESS

The Static of the Spheres is a work of fiction. The characters, incidents, dialogues, settings, events, and organizations portrayed in it are products of the author's imagination or are used fictionally and are not to be construed as real.

Manufactured in the United States of America

Illustration on page 29 by George Ulrich

Design and cover photograph by Eric Kraft

www.erickraft.com

First published in the United States by Apple-Wood Books

First Babbington Press Edition: October 2008

ISBN: 978-1-105-74737-3

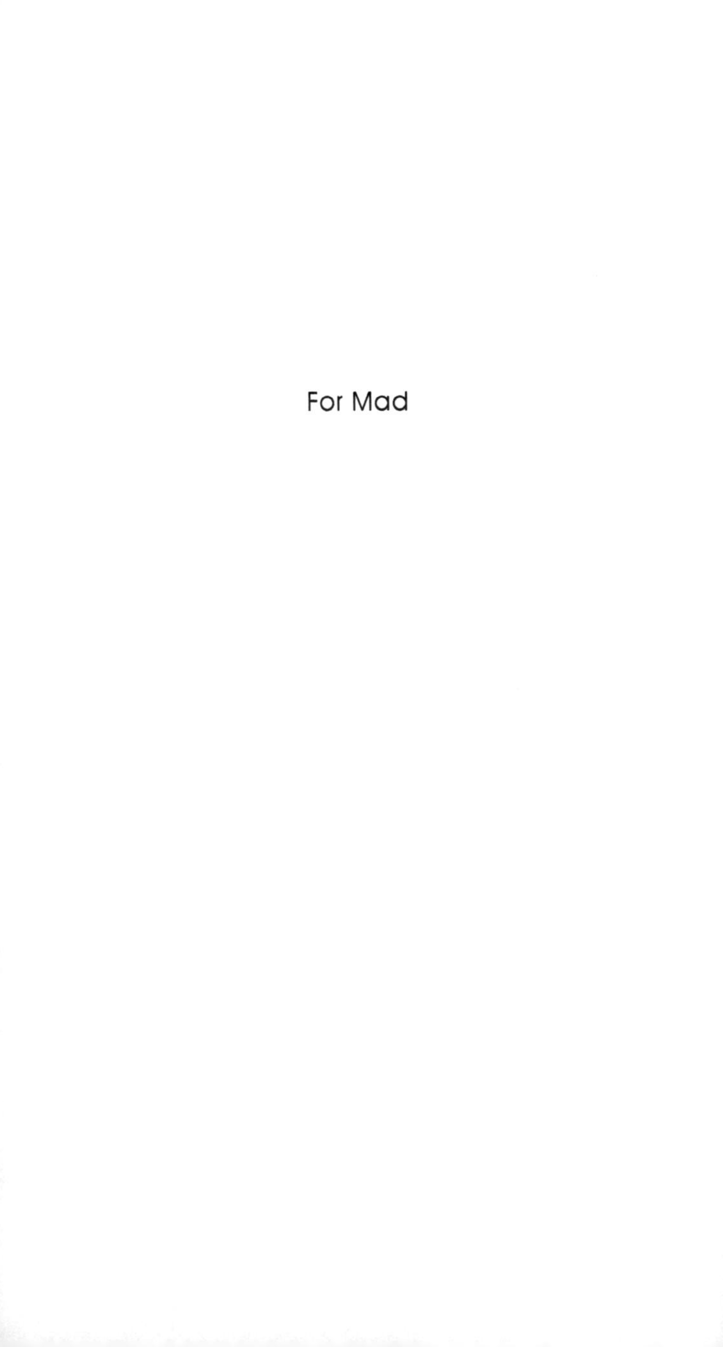

For Mad

The Static of the Spheres

(A Memoir with Inventions)

Peter Leroy

THE BABBINGTON PRESS

We are all obliged, if we are to make reality endurable, to nurse a few little follies in ourselves.

Marcel Proust
Within a Budding Grove
(translated by C. K. Scott Moncrieff)

Preface

OF THE DIFFICULTIES that arose during the writing of "The Static of the Spheres," no other posed so intriguing a set of challenges as the need to create a preoccupation for Guppa, something that he could do in his living room of an evening, in the quiet hours after dinner, that would be the equivalent of his practicing culling clams.

Guppa's clam-culling skills were legendary. When he had worked on the line at the clam-packing plant, he had been an inspiration to anyone who worked beside him, and at the annual Clam Fests he had won the culling competition for twelve years in succession, a record that stands to this day. When he became foreman of the culling section and retired from active day-in-and-day-out culling, he practiced at home in the evenings to keep his hand in, so that when a new culler joined the crew or when Guppa thought that the work was slowing, he could step over to the galvanized table where the clams were dumped and put on a display of speed and accuracy that was still dazzling, still inspiring.

So that he could practice at home, in the privacy of his own living room, while listening to the radio, and later while watching television, he would arrange in a semicircle in front of his favorite comfy chair a set of peck baskets into which, while blindfolded—or at least, during the television years, without looking—he would toss clams that were randomly arranged in a bushel basket between his feet. Arranging the clams randomly again after Guppa had culled them became my job as soon as I was old enough to perform it.

At first, immediately after Guppa had retired from active culling, he had used clams straight from the bay, but these quickly became too smelly for Gumma to tolerate. For her part, Gumma liked to spend an evening curled up on the sofa with a slide rule and a book of recreational mathematics problems, very much as I have described in the pages that follow. She said that the stink of the clams made it hard for her to think straight, that the clams reeked and her head reeled. So Guppa and I undertook a project that threw us together for long and happy hours in the cellar, at his workbench. We constructed practice clams. Guppa would open the clams and remove the edible portion. I would scrape the insides of the shells clean and wash and dry them thoroughly. Together we mixed mortar to use as ballast in each clam, so that the heft would be realistic. Guppa measured varying amounts of the mortar for each clam, so that each would vary a bit from the average weight for clams their size, which Gumma calculated, throwing herself into the problem with great intensity, covering sheets of paper with notes and numbers. Guppa spooned the right amount of mortar into a clean valve, and then after the mortar was dry I glued the opposite valve to it.

The memories of the time that we spent in the cellar, working together, are among the most pleasant of my childhood. I would gladly have related them just as they were, and would probably have called this work "The Cement Clams," but in "My Mother Takes a Tumble" I had made Guppa a Studebaker salesman rather than a foreman in the culling section of the clam-packing plant, and now I felt that I was stuck with that story, just as I found myself stuck with the little lie about the hard candies that my great-grandmother offered me in "Do Clams Bite?" So, I worked out a comparable kind of practice for a Studebaker salesman of the first rank: categorizing potential buyers according to the sales pitch most likely to succeed with each—culling of another sort.

So far, so good. I thought that I would call this "All in the Cards." Ah, but then when I tried to imagine Guppa and my ten-year-old self passing happy hours in the cellar at work filling out note cards, I realized that it was not a project that would have held my attention for the long periods that constructing practice clams had, and so I cast about for something else that Guppa and I could do together in the cellar. I put myself back in Gumma and Guppa's living room and looked around for something that might inspire me. To my surprise and relief, the solution came to me at once. I found myself twisting the dials on Gumma's magnificent multi-band radio and wishing that I had one like it. Guppa and I would build a shortwave radio.

THE SECOND MOST VEXING PROBLEM arose after I wrote the sentence that now stands as the last one in the bathroom scene. At once, I began to have misgivings about the whole scene. I meant to go on, and I meant to be quite frank, but I hesitated, because I realized that the scene would succeed only if it were at once frank and delicate. I didn't want to seem prudish, but I didn't want to embarrass myself either. I didn't want to describe the bathtub shenanigans that I had concocted for Eliza and me in a way that would mean injuring Eliza or disturbing the perilous balance that I had in mind for this work.

I went downstairs to the lobby, where Albertine was behind the desk, working on the accounts. I lit a cigarette and began pacing up and down. Al didn't look up. I began sighing whenever I passed the desk, but still she didn't look up. I began muttering "damn-damn-damn" under my breath. Al put her pencil down and leaned on the desk.

"Okay," she said. "I hear you. What's the matter?"

"Oh, I don't know," I said.

"I'll give you two minutes," she said. She went back to work.

After about a minute and a half, I said, "Well, I'm having doubts about a scene in which Eliza is giving me a bath. I think it's very important, because it leads to the confusion of motives for my wanting the shortwave radio—the mixture of sexual desire, jealousy, pride, anger, and my simple ingenuous hankering for a shortwave radio. But I'm afraid that if it isn't handled just right it will look like an unnecessary sex scene and that it will embarrass Eliza to boot."

"Why don't you ask Eliza what she thinks?" she suggested.

My jaw dropped. Al and I have been married for more than twenty years, but still there are times when I am not sure whether she possesses a surpassing understanding, an uncanny percipience, or is just not listening to me most of the time.

"There is no Eliza," I said. "I made her up."

Al looked at me as if I were a nitwit and went back to work. I trudged back upstairs. At least half an hour passed before I decided what to do. I dialed the desk from the phone in my workroom.

"Small's Hotel," answered Al.

"Al," I said. "Will you be Eliza?"

"Will you take me to lunch?" she asked.

"Okay," I said.

"Sure," said Al.

I TELEPHONED ELIZA AT ONCE to invite her to have lunch with me. Eliza is now sixty-three. After Dudley Beaker died, she stayed on in the stucco house on No Bridge Road, at the end of which there is now a bridge.

"Hello?" she said, in the small and tentative tone she uses to answer the phone, as if she expected a call from a creditor or a grasping relative.

"Eliza," I said. "It's Peter."

"Peter, darling," she said, switching at once to the voice she uses with friends, a voice like velvet or cognac or *pot de crême*.

"Eliza, will you have lunch with me?" I asked.

"Oh, I think that would be delightful," she said. "When would that be?"

"How about one-thirty?"

"Oh, you mean today."

"Yes."

"Oh, well, yes, fine. I wonder if I have anything that I can wear? I'm standing here in a Chinese robe. You don't think I could wear that, do you? No. I know what, why don't you and the gorgeous Albertine come here, and I will fix you some lunch?"

My heart stopped for a moment, though I was certain that the offer wasn't genuine.

"Nonsense!" I said. "I insist that I take you out somewhere—just you and me. Al is otherwise engaged."

I held my breath.

"Oh, well," she said. "Fine. I think I can put some outfit together."

I let a long sigh out to one side of the mouthpiece, and I was sure that I could hear a similar sigh from the other end of the line. Both of us were relieved. None of the domestic arts was ever an interest of Eliza's, because, she said to me once, "Not one of those activities gets you anywhere. After cleaning a house, you're merely back to where you were before the place got dirty. After you've cooked, eaten, and cleaned up after Thursday's meal, you can't say that you are anywhere but where you were after you had cooked, eaten, and cleaned up after Wednesday's meal."

I suggested that we eat at the Manifest Destiny Diner, a favorite haunt of mine, which I like for its Wild West motif, its thick 'n' juicy Vanishing Buffaloburgers, and its frosty mugs o' beer, but she wanted to try Pussy's, a new place downtown, where the sign that directs one to the toilets says Litter Boxes, a hamburger is called a Cat's Meow, soup is served in heavy earthenware bowls that say CAT on the side, and the staff smiles relentlessly.

"Something from the bar?" asked a waitress, before we had quite settled in.

"Yes indeed," said Eliza. "Drinks."

The waitress smiled but did not laugh.

"Vodka and soda," said Eliza. "No ice."

"I'll have a martini," I said. "Straight up, with an olive."

Al stepped out of character for a moment. "I'll have the same," she said, "but with a twist. Forget the vodka and soda."

While we were having our drinks, Eliza read what I had written so far of the bathroom scene. She handed the manuscript back to me and asked me to order her another vodka and soda. She winked when she said it, so I ordered her another martini. She asked, "Well, Peter, what comes after this?"

"That's what I wanted to ask you," I said.

The waitress brought Eliza's drink, and I decided that I'd have another too.

"Well," said Eliza, "of course, it's up to you, but I think that, if I were you, I would not include anything explicitly erotic. I would think that it would be much—better—more effective—to just provide pretty much what you have—or maybe just a little more—some disconnected sensory details that would invite the reader to imagine an erotic—situation—taking either your part or mine—*chacun à son goût,* don't you think? Just mention in a list—say—the smooth, wet, and slippery body of a boy of—ten, I think—a cotton blouse, damp with steam, clinging to the breasts of a voluptuous woman of thirty-four—her blond hair pinned up—a strand or two falling over her forehead—droplets of steam on the mirror and the white tiles—the tiny sound of popping bubbles—millions of tiny popping bubbles—hissing and crackling—like champagne or static—muffled by the clouds of steam—the light diffused by the steam—vague highlights on the boy's smooth, wet skin—her hands in the warm water—the warm water enveloping the boy's body—the slick, smooth skin along his thighs—his wet hand along her arm— the rounded tops of her quite lovely breasts when she leans over the edge of the tub—the firm pressure of the tub against her belly—her hand brushing against his smooth thigh—that sort of thing."

THEN CAME THE THIRD PROBLEM: the flood. I had nearly finished the manuscript when nature interrupted my work and divided my attention. Most of the material was there, though a few things were still out of place and there were still some unanswered questions and some voices that I could not quite hear clearly. Rain began falling one night and continued to fall for eight days. Throughout that time, Babbington was nearly invisible: it was only a set of vague gray shapes beyond the rain. The water level in the cellar of the hotel rose steadily, and there was nothing we could do to stop it. We worked for hours each day bringing endangered tools, supplies, and mementos up to the safety of the ground floor. I was so concerned that my jars of nuts and bolts and the like would be disorganized that I insisted that we place things around the hotel in the same positions that they had occupied in the cellar. When the waters receded, I set up in the cellar every fan that we had, and in a couple of days the place was more or less back to normal. We carried everything back to the cellar and arranged it as it had been.

Then only the last and most perilous of the difficulties was still to be overcome: doubt. It was as if, while I was distracted by the flood, Fat Hank had moved into my workroom.

At about the time that I began work on "The Static of the Spheres," Albertine brought home two large cartons of wood from which she planned to build a miniature of Small's Hotel. She had in mind a true miniature, not just a representation of the exterior. She would build with miniature framing, tiny nails, sheathing, and clapboards. Best of all, she had bought a set of tiny, precise tools: a square, a plane, saws with teensy teeth, a mitre box, and so on.

She was at work on her small hotel throughout my work on this, and I suppose that the rhythms of her miniature construction—the tap-tap-tap of her little hammer, the back-and-forth whisper of her little saw—underlie some passages. But that is by the way; I want to say something about the materials themselves.

When she brought all the stuff home, we spread it out neatly on the tabletops in the dining room and spent quite a while just handling all of it and looking at it.

"You know, Al," I said to her, "this is just like the moment when Guppa has all the parts of the radio lined up on his workbench. I have the same anticipatory feelings, the same mixture of excitement, eagerness—and fear. I sense, in all this cute stuff you brought home, what I should sense in the parts of the radio when they lie in ranks on Guppa's workbench—the presence of a potential magnificence, something that I've found in the parts of other things before they're assembled. The components might be—oh—a clutter of memories, boxes full of thin slabs of basswood and slender dowels, or ranks of vacuum tubes, resistors, capacitors, transformers, and the like. Sleeping in these things is the capacity to become a book, a dollhouse, or a shortwave receiver. One has the feeling that merely by gathering the parts, one has made a step toward realizing the end.

"'Ah,' one is tempted to say, 'the pieces are all there. Now all I have to do is put them together.'

"But—" I said, dramatically, "—it may be better, sometimes, to leave the pieces as they are, unassembled, for the potential book crackles with wit, the shutters on the potential dollhouse are straight, and the signals picked up by the potential receiver are clear and strong, but the actual book is going to have its passages of half-baked philosophy and weepy sentimentality, some of the shutters on the actual dollhouse will hang at odd angles, and the receiver may bring in nothing but a rising and falling howl muffled by a thick hiss."

Al laughed at me and told me to get upstairs and get to work, and I did.

Peter Leroy
Small's Island
March 18, 1983

1

AT HOME, in my parents' house in Babbington Heights, in the corner of the attic that was my bedroom, I had, on a table beside my bed, a small Philco radio. It was made of cream-colored plastic. The radio had seen years of use on somebody else's bedside table before I got it for my room. Over the years, the heat from the bulb that lighted its dial had discolored and cracked the plastic in a spot along the rounded edge of the top, right above the dial. On winter nights, when the attic was cold, I would bring the radio close to me, onto the bed, under the covers, and rest one hand on the warm, discolored spot while I listened.

Of all the programs that I listened to on that radio, I can remember only one clearly: one about a boy about my age who lost everyone who was dear to him—his mother and father and grandparents and a clever younger sister with a voice like a flute—in a shipwreck, and was left alone, entirely alone, on an island somewhere warm and wet and windy, and called out for them in the night, calling against the persistent, overpowering sound of the wind and the sea, and listened in despair for the sound of their voices through the crashing surf and howling wind. I huddled in my bed, with the blankets pulled over my head, and trembled when the sound of his voice and the wind filled the little cave that I had made. This program so terrified me that I wanted to cry out for my own parents, to run downstairs for some comfort from them, at least to reassure myself that they were still there, but I couldn't run to them because I was listening to the radio at a time of night when my mother didn't allow me to listen, since the programs that were broadcast at those late hours were, she had told me often enough, the sort of thing that scared the wits out of young boys.

Though I remember only that one program, I can remember as clearly as a memorized poem or a popular song the susurrous and crackling static that accompanied everything I heard on the little radio. Over the course of time, this insistent sound has pushed its way from the background of my radio memories to the foreground, and the private detectives, shipwrecked travelers, cowboys, bandleaders, and comedians who once were able to shout over it now call out only faintly and indecipherably, like voices calling against the roaring of the sea and the wind.

Then Guppa bought a Motorola console radio as a Christmas gift for Gumma, and at once the Philco became a pedestrian radio. The Motorola had several bands, and it could pull in programs from places so far removed from Babbington that their names alone, printed at intervals along the dial, were enough to bring to mind notions of places so remote and exotic that I had to work to convince myself that they were real places, places where people worked, slept, ate meals, listened to radios, places that I could, someday, actually visit: Balbec, London, Macondo, Moscow, Paris, Tokyo. It was as if the Motorola were more worldly, more sophisticated, more knowledgeable than the Philco, as if the Philco were naive, untraveled, because it knew only Babbington and the surrounding towns and cities that everyone knew. Not only could the Philco not detect the signals from far-flung places, but it seemed to me that the little radio was ignorant of the notion that these places even existed.

2

AS SOON AS I HAD LISTENED to Gumma's Motorola, I wanted—no, I needed—a more sophisticated radio. It was a familiar sequence: seeing the lack of something, one feels the need for it.

Even now, when I have reached an age when, I tell myself, I should be beyond such feelings, I find myself in the grip, now and then, of an irresistible desire to replace a perfectly good turntable, amplifier, or tuner with a newer and more complicated one. I consider myself, on the whole, a mature and sensible fellow, and I expend no little effort in trying to talk myself out of these periodic attacks of electronic lust, but—as Porky White has said to me so often—"Look, it's like a fight. One guy comes into the ring in a gray pin-striped robe and across the back in small black letters it says REASON. He's wearing glasses, and his hair is thinning. Into the opposite corner leaps a guy in a robe of scarlet satin, and across the back in orange and purple letters it says THE IRRESISTIBLE URGE. He looks like a bull, and there's foam at the corners of his mouth. Where you gonna put your money, kid?"

Still, I think that, even at ten, I might have talked myself into being content with the little Philco if I had not spent the New Year's Eve that followed with Dudley Beaker and Eliza Foote at Gumma and Guppa's, and my desire had not become so mixed up with other, baser emotions—lust and pride—that I could not separate them, as one sometimes cannot separate the overlapping signals of weak radio stations.

3

IT WAS NOT UNUSUAL for Eliza and Mr. Beaker to look after me for an evening when I was spending a weekend at Gumma and Guppa's. For many years, they would stay with me on Saturday nights while Gumma and Guppa went out to play bridge with friends.

I was, throughout my childhood, required to take a bath sometime between dinner and bedtime, and Eliza took on the responsibility of bathing me when she and Mr. Beaker were taking care of me on one of those Saturday nights during my earliest years. Mr. Beaker left this responsibility to her gladly, and he would spend my bath time in the living room, smoking his pipe and reading. Eliza invented a number of bath time games over the years. My favorite of these was making soapsuds landscapes. We would work up a lather of suds in the tub together, enough so that the suds covered the water entirely. We would spend some time smoothing the layer of suds so that it completely and evenly covered the water, with the exception, of course, of the spot where I, sitting, projected through the layer of suds. Then, moving and shaping the suds with our hands, we would create a landscape around me. There might be mountains in the distance near my feet, a winding road, conical evergreens, a river. The renderings of the features were never very precise, and they began to decay as soon as they were constructed, from the bursting of the soap bubbles and the pull of gravity. By the time the little village in the valley had been constructed, for example, the mountains had sunk to the level of the plain, and the river would be nearly indistinguishable. To appreciate a completed soapscape, one had to be able to see the mountains as they had been when they were new and to imagine that they were better formed than they really were.

As I grew and aged, the pleasure that I took in soapsuds landscapes and Eliza's other bathtub games began, as one might expect, to shift from the aesthetic to the erotic.

On that important New Year's Eve, my parents were going to a celebration in our neighborhood, and Gumma and Guppa were going to some kind of wingding that someone in their set was throwing, perhaps a New Year's Eve bridge tournament. When Eliza learned about their plans, she volunteered to stay with me at Gumma and Guppa's.

"We won't be going anywhere anyway," she told Gumma. "Dudley thinks that New Year's Eve celebrations are not at all the right way to usher in the new year. He says that in the Orient people make a point of planning, as the old year wanes, what endeavors they wish to undertake in the coming year, and then in the first moments of the new year they do a lick of work on each of these undertakings, thereby ensuring that they will prosper throughout the year, and this, he feels, is a much wiser way of beginning a year than a lot of drunken whoopdedo."

So it was that on New Year's Eve Eliza and I were in the bathroom, shaping a soapsuds landscape, while Dudley was in the living room, making a list of endeavors that he hoped would prosper in the coming year. Eliza and I had been at work for a while. The room was steamy. Droplets covered the mirror and the chrome fixtures. The droplets commingled and grew and ran suddenly down erratic courses. Eliza's cheeks were rosy with the heat. Damp strands of her blond hair fell across her eyes. She blew up at them to get them out of her way or pushed them up with the back of her hand, keeping the soap out of her eyes. She bent over the tub, working at shaping the soapsuds. Her damp blouse clung to her breasts. Her hand grazed my thigh while she was shaping suds into a peasant cottage, and we glanced at each other simultaneously. There was a look in her eyes that I had never seen before.

4

FLUSHED AND GIGGLY, Eliza and I returned to the living room after my bath and settled ourselves in front of the new radio. I was wearing a white terrycloth robe. Eliza tousled my hair and hugged my shoulders. Mr. Beaker looked up from his lists, acknowledged us with a smile, and went back to work.

Eliza turned the radio on, and she began twisting the dial, exploring for signals. For much of the time while she explored, she was between stations, and the living room was full of the noises that lie between stations on a radio dial, noises that are drowned out when we come upon a strong signal. Some of those noises come from within the receiver itself, produced by the operation of the receiver's circuits, noises from within the machine. Other noises come from outside the receiver. The sources of some of those are local, familiar, homely. These may, for example, be produced by the ignition systems of passing Studebakers or by the motor in a refrigerator or by a toaster. The sources of others, however, are distant, exotic, intriguing. These may, for example, be produced by stations too far away for a clear signal to reach us, stations calling from God knows where, with voices as weak as that of a boy calling against the wind. Or they may originate in electrical discharges from the sun, from other stars, other galaxies: the pervasive and indecipherable, eternal and inestimable noise, the static of the spheres.

While Eliza and I are curled up on the floor twiddling the dial, searching for a signal, let me pause for a moment to plant in your mind the notion that our senses, like radio receivers, pick up lots of noise, and that in our perception of events the truth is sometimes nearly buried by static. Let me suggest, too, that in remembering the things that have happened to us, the people who have spoken to us, the things that they have said, we introduce new static, and that as time goes by we may even find, as I did with the whine from my little Philco, that the noise has become stronger than the signal.

"Oh, I know what we can do," cried Eliza suddenly. "We can follow the new year as it approaches us, and then follow it across the country."

"Calm down, you two," said Mr. Beaker. He stood up from his work and stretched. He chuckled indulgently. "You seem quite worked up. Look at you. You're flushed and giggly."

Eliza looked at me and reddened a little more. So did I. We giggled again. Mr. Beaker walked over beside us and rumpled Eliza's hair. He took another log from the wood box and drew back the mesh curtain that hung in front of the fire.

"Peter," said Mr. Beaker. His back was toward us. He was working at the fire, using tongs to rearrange the logs. There was, it seemed to me, something stern, something menacing in his voice.

"Yes?" I answered. The word leaped from me like a small frightened animal. My heart began to beat quickly, and my voice seemed to tremble. I threw a wild look at Eliza. She made a motion with both hands, as if pushing against a plump, resilient pillow of air, and I could tell at once that she meant, "Slow down. Calm down." I cleared my throat, and asked again, in a steadier voice, "Yes?"

Mr. Beaker spun around to look at me. The fire blazed suddenly, and the room filled with its heat. Perspiration formed on my forehead and upper lip. "Is something wrong with you, Peter?" he asked. "You sound odd. You almost sound frightened."

I smiled at him. The smile was meant to be that smile of amused incredulity that we adults have learned to affect when we are caught doing something that we shouldn't. For some reason, we continue to expect that smile to work for us, even though, as soon as we see it on anyone else, we say to ourselves, "This guy is as guilty as sin." I thought that I had shaped it pretty well, but Mr. Beaker's look remained one of concern, and when I look at this scene now in my mind's eye, the smile on my face, the trembling lips, the blinking eyes look as if they belong on a plucky fellow with a noose around his neck.

Mr. Beaker reached toward me suddenly. I raised my hands to ward off the blow that I thought was coming. He reached between my hands and felt my forehead.

"I think he's running a fever," he said to Eliza.

"Oh, it's nothing," she said. "He's still warm from his bath. The whole room was—steamy—very steamy—in there." She took Mr. Beaker's hand and held it against her own forehead. "See?" she asked. "I'm a little overheated myself."

Mr. Beaker smiled and caressed Eliza's forehead. He leaned forward and kissed the top of her head.

"I was thinking, Peter," he said, turning to me, "that you ought to do as I am doing. You should decide what you would like to accomplish in the coming year and then, as the year turns, make some small start toward accomplishing it."

"Maybe he already has," said Eliza. She looked steadily at me for a moment. The fire was yellow and bright. It flared again, and the heat rushed over me. I thought that there was a good chance that I would either faint or throw up if I didn't do something—move around a bit, take some deep breaths. I stood up quickly, as if inspired by Mr. Beaker's suggestion.

"That's right!" I cried. "You know what I want? I want—" I had spoken too quickly. I had a few ideas about what I wanted—vague ideas, certainly, but ideas just the same—but of the ones that came to mind, none were things that I could announce, or confess, to Mr. Beaker. I certainly could not have said to him, "I want Eliza," and if somehow I had found it possible to say that, I would not have known how to say to him why I wanted Eliza or exactly what for. My mind hissed and crackled, much like a radio between stations. Now and then a strong, but inexpressible, desire came through as I looked wildly around the room, and at last, to my relief, something came through strong and clear: Gumma's radio. "—I want a radio like this," I said.

"That's good, Peter," said Mr. Beaker, beaming. "Now you have a goal. Of course, a radio like this is a little beyond your reach, but it is a good sign, I think, that you set your goal high. Now let's see if we can bring it down to a point where you can, if you extend yourself, if you really stretch out, grasp it. How would you like a small radio that you could keep on a bedside table at home? If you were to begin working at odd jobs—"

"I already have a radio on my bedside table at home," I said. A great many emotions had run through me while Mr. Beaker had been talking. First, there was passion, a passion that I could not express because there was no acceptable object for it. Then there was fear, the fear that the passion would be discovered if I didn't hide it somehow. Next there was pride, pride that arose when Mr. Beaker told me that a radio like Gumma's was a little beyond my reach, as if he were saying that a woman, a grown woman like Eliza, was a little beyond my reach. And then there was surprise, for I discovered after I had said it that I really did want a radio like Gumma's. I now burned with a desire for such a radio, so passionate a desire that it surpassed anything I had felt for Eliza.

"Ah," said Mr. Beaker, "but suppose that you were to build a radio yourself. That would be something quite different from the radio that you have at home."

If I were responding to that remark now, I would say, "No, it wouldn't, Dudley. It would be essentially the same: it would be the same in purpose and in function. It would pull in the same frightening programs about shipwrecked boys, the same music, the same comedy programs, and I have no doubt that it would pull in the same annoying static. I know why you said what you did, Dudley, and I'm surprised, surprised and disappointed, for I know that what made you make that remark was the same crazy idea that inspires those people who praise a thing—a dining-room table, say—simply because someone has made it himself, attaching to it a value that is not derived from any improvement in form or function over any other dining-room table, a value derived merely from the way in which it was made. What did you take me for, an idiot? I may have been just a kid, but I could see, even then, that any radio that I would build for myself, if I could even imagine building a radio for myself, would differ from the little Philco at home only in being a sloppier job."

At the time, however, I said, "I want a radio that gets different programs."

Mr. Beaker began an elaborately simple explanation of the way a radio works, apparently thinking, from my remark, that I imagined that the programs I heard on the radio came from within the radio, and that a different radio would, simply because it was a different radio, play different programs.

"Dudley," interrupted Eliza, "I think you misinterpreted Peter's remark, and I think you're underestimating his understanding."

"Oh?" said Mr. Beaker. "Am I, Peter?"

"Yeah," I said. "What I meant is that my radio at home can't get all the programs that this radio can get."

"Oh, well—" said Mr. Beaker.

Ah, Beaker, I wish I had you here now. The conversation would be considerably different today from what it was then.

"As I see it, Dudley," I would say, "a radio is a lot like a pair of ears. With my ears, I can't hear everything that there is to hear. For one thing, my ears aren't sensitive enough. Some things are too quiet for me to hear most of the time—for instance, the cat's stomach. Usually, I don't hear the cat's stomach at all, but if I lie on the floor and put my ear right against the cat's stomach, I can hear a sort of wheezing and rumbling."

"That's not a good idea, Peter," you would say. "Cats generally have fleas—"

"There's another example," I'd interrupt. "Fleas make noise too, but we don't hear them. Little bits of dust crashing into each other when they float in the air would make a hell of a racket if we could hear them."

"I see what you—"

"Other sounds," I'd say, firmly, "are too far away to hear. My equipment—my receiving set of ears—is not powerful enough to pick them up. You and I and Eliza, while we were sitting in the living room that New Year's Eve, knew that Gumma and Guppa were probably laughing and telling stories or playing bridge at the same time, but we couldn't hear their laughter or their stories or the snap of the cards, could we?"

"Of course not. We—"

"And in the farthest reaches of the heavens, in distant galaxies, stars were exploding, but we couldn't hear those either, could we?"

"No."

"And, more important than any of that, something was happening to Albertine at that time, at that very moment when you and I were going on about the radio, someone was talking to her, or she was thinking about something, or dreaming about something—something was happening to her, Dudley, that would contribute to making her the sweetie she is today, and we didn't know anything about it. There was no apparatus that would allow us to tune in to the Albertine Show and find out what was happening to her."

Heh-heh-heh. Oh, I am rolling now, Dud. I can feel myself taking the upper hand, I can feel your grip loosening with each word. Where was I? I did sensitivity. I did power. Range. Range.

"Finally, Dudley," I would say, "some sounds are outside the range of frequencies of sound that my ears can pick up, just as—"

"Calm down, Peter—"

"—just as some stations were outside the range of the little Philco. Do you understand?"

"I understand."

But at the time, Mr. Beaker just went on and said, "—then what you want is a shortwave radio."

"I do?" I said, playing the part of naive child as well as it has ever been played.

"Yes, of course," said Mr. Beaker. "With a shortwave radio, you will be able to pick up conversations among people all over the globe. You'll hear the babble of many tongues. You may even pick up a few useful phrases."

He was right, and I knew it, and the prospect of making contact with all the mysterious people out there sold me at once on the idea of a shortwave radio, a radio that would allow me to eavesdrop on the conversations of people in all the quaint countries I had heard about, people whose habitual preoccupations I had come to understand from the phrases that I had heard repeated about them, phrases that classified them according to their national passions: Japanese beetles, French bread, Irish coffee, Spanish fly, Mexican jumping beans, Chinese checkers, British steel, German beer, Russian roulette, Canadian sunsets, Turkish taffy, Swiss cheese, Italian loafers, Polish jokes, Hungarian goulash, Cuban cigars, Siamese twins, Panama hats, Greek statues, Dutch uncles.

5

"GUPPA COULD build me a radio," I said.

"I'm sure he could," said Mr. Beaker. He turned toward Eliza, and from the way his ear twitched, and from the flash of anger in Eliza's eyes, I knew that he had winked.

"And I could help him," I said, through clenched teeth.

"I'm sure you could," said Mr. Beaker. He began loading his pipe. He wore a small, twisted grin. It was not until several years later that I learned the word *supercilious,* but when I did, I found that I already knew exactly what it meant.

I was furious. Mr. Beaker took his pipe tool from his pocket and began tamping his tobacco. If I had been holding the poker, I might have hit him with it. Instead, it occurred to me to use another weapon: Eliza.

"You know, Mr. Beaker," I began, in a tone that startled me, "Eliza and I—"

Eliza had been looking into the fire. Now she snapped her head around to look at me, and there was on her face an expression of terror so striking that my throat caught when I saw it. She looked as frightened and helpless as I imagine the marooned boy in the radio program must have looked when he realized that he was alone. A chill ran through me, and I actually shuddered. Instantly I lost all desire to hurt Mr. Beaker, because I wanted instead to comfort Eliza.

"Eliza and I could look through Guppa's magazines," I said, looking into her eyes as I said it. "I bet one of them tells how to make a shortwave radio."

Mr. Beaker looked at his watch. "I think it's a little late for that sort of thing," he said. "You really should be in bed."

"My mother said that I could stay up until midnight," I said.

"And you have," said Mr. Beaker. "It's twelve-eighteen."

6

I PROPOSED the project to Guppa the very next night, while he and Gumma and I were sitting in the living room after dinner.

Guppa was working on what he called his pigeonholes. One reason that Guppa was so phenomenally successful a Studebaker salesman was that he developed individual sales pitches to suit each potential customer. He didn't wait for those potential customers to walk into the showroom, either; he went right out into the field after them and ran them down. In later years, I realized that Big Grandfather was disdainful of Guppa's occupation because it was so definitely landbound, just as my father was landbound in his gas station, and I know that Big Grandfather didn't think much of that. He would snort at the mention of anything automotive. Guppa, however, considered the hunt for Studebaker buyers every bit as exciting and demanding as the hunt for clams. If it wasn't man pitted against nature, it was man pitted against man, and the reluctant Studebaker buyer could be a warier and more elusive prey than the wily bivalve.

To make certain that no potential buyer was overlooked, Guppa kept a card file with information about everyone in Babbington who might eventually be made, in one way or another, to become a Studebaker owner. Guppa had a lot of confidence in himself and in Studebakers. He would eliminate a person from the file only if he was convinced that there was no hope whatsoever of an eventual sale. I know, for instance, that he kept a small stack of cards with the names of the crippled and blind in the pocket of his Sunday suit, and he would take these out after communion and say a silent prayer for the cure of each.

Guppa believed that every one of the people in his active file would buy a car from him sooner or later, and that belief was the real secret of his success. It was, as he saw it, just a matter of catching the prey at the right moment or using the right lure.

Of an evening, Guppa would set himself up in the living room to do his pigeonholes. He would bring a straightback chair in from the dining room and put it in front of his comfortable chair. On the seat of the straightback chair he would prop a large, shallow, cardboard carton that had in it a number of compartments formed by interlocking cardboard dividers. This carton might have been used originally to ship apples or glassware or electrical equipment. Guppa would sit in his comfortable chair, listening to the radio, or, in later years, watching television, and pull out a batch of his cards. He'd shuffle them, turn the top card, read his notes on it, and mull the situation over. After some time, he'd come to a decision about the prospects for selling a Studebaker to the person described on the card. He'd deal the card into one of the pigeonholes in the cardboard carton. Each pigeonhole represented a strategy. They were labeled in Guppa's wavy style of block lettering. Some of the labels made sense to me, but others made sense only to Guppa:

THE IRON IS HOT
WAIT 'N' SEE
RATTLE SKELETON
PROD
WHEEDLE
CAJOLE

and so on. It looked like fun, this process of pigeonholing Babbingtonians. I had a small part in it. As soon as I was able to handle the cards without damaging them, Guppa would let me scramble their order for him. He liked to begin his pigeonholing afresh every month or so, yanking all the cards out of their holes, scrambling them, and reconsidering each. He would pull all the cards out of their pigeonholes and give them to me. My job was to put them into random order. Since I wasn't nimble-fingered enough to shuffle them, I would spread them out all over the living room floor and then walk around picking the cards up in another order. I got into the habit of squatting to read the cards as I went along, and this habit has stayed with me throughout my life. Now, when I am about to do some painting and squat to begin spreading newspapers on the floor, or when I am building a fire and squat to stuff a crumpled sheet of newspaper under the kindling, something comes over me with the act of squatting, something left from the days when I used to rearrange Guppa's cards, and I begin to read whatever article is in front of me, reading for that small but useful piece of information about a person that would have held the key to the sale of another Studebaker.

I was pleased and thrilled to discover, the first time I did this work for Guppa, that there was a card for me, with my own name lettered across the top in Guppa's wavy block letters.

After the cards had been randomized, Guppa would spend evenings during the next month going through them and reconsidering each one. As soon as I was able to print neatly enough to satisfy Guppa, I got even more responsibility: Guppa would save the birth announcements and obituary notices from the *Babbington Reporter,* and I made out cards for new-born Babbingtonians and drew black borders around the cards of the deceased. Guppa didn't discard the dead prospects' cards, however. He used them to warm up before he got down to serious pigeonholing, pulling a card or two from the stack of black-bordered ones and thinking about what he *might* have done to snare the pigeon before he or she had dropped off. Now and then during these warmups, he would heave a sigh and his eyes would mist over if the sense of loss or of lost opportunity became too great.

I also copied the data from old, worn, and dirty cards onto clean new ones. This work, which I did for several years, spending some time on it whenever I visited Gumma and Guppa, gave me some familiarity with a large random sample of people in Babbington, at least with many of those who were even remotely likely to purchase a Studebaker someday.

While Guppa was working with his pigeonholes, Gumma liked to pass the time manipulating large numbers with one of her slide rules. Gumma's affection for the slide rule began when she took an off-season job in one of the slide-rule factories in Hargrove. She had worked at one job or another for nearly all her married life, but her work at the slide-rule factory was, as far as I knew, the first that she had ever really enjoyed. Before that, she had worked because Guppa was either selling too many Studebakers or too few. When he was selling too few, she worked to bring the income up to the budget, and when he was selling too many, she worked to help him keep up with the demand. Selling Studebakers in Babbington was a seasonal business, like clamming. Since the economy of Babbington was so dependent on the clam and clam by-products, such as gewgaws and driveway topping, most businesses in Babbington slipped into a torpor in the winter, when the bay was cold and choppy, and the air stung, and fewer clammies were at work. With fewer clams coming in, the work at the Babbington Clam packing plant and at Bivalve By-products, the by-product plant, would slow. Less money circulated around town, and most shopkeepers stood at their windows most of the day, looking at one another across the slushy streets. Most people in Babbington, in every line of work, expected this winter lull and considered whatever work they did seasonal. Only a few occupations—schoolteaching and bartending come to mind—provided steady, reliable employment throughout the winter, and the few people in these occupations were courted during the cold months by anyone who tried to make a living selling something. Only Guppa, the most senior of the salesmen at Babbington Studebaker, worked the year round; the others did one thing or another to make ends meet during the winter. And even Guppa, skilled as he was, found the pickings lean during the cold months. So, Gumma worked during the winter to help make ends meet.

During the summer, on the other hand, when the sun was strong and the breezes were warm, the ranks of clammies would be swollen by vacationing college students, moonlighting milkmen, and many others. The clam-packing plant would go onto three shifts, working day and night, and a person could find work there just by showing up at almost any time. Then Babbington bustled, people felt flush, and Guppa would say that selling a Studebaker was as easy as shooting fish in a barrel, although when I asked him how exactly shooting fish in a barrel was done and how the fish got into the barrel in the first place, he admitted that he had never tried shooting fish in a barrel and that it might actually be pretty difficult for all he knew. During the summer, Babbington Studebaker would take on extra help, and Gumma often pitched in then just to help Guppa out.

However, as soon as she began working on slide rules, Gumma fell in love with them, and she worked at a slide rule factory year-round for many years thereafter. A slide rule, which is today merely a curiosity, a relic of a simpler and cruder past, the mechanical analogue of an electronic calculator, has three main parts: the stock, the slide, and the cursor (see diagram).

Gumma was fondest of the cursor. From her first off-season job installing screws in the shiny little metal frame that holds the cursor in place on the stock, she had worked her way up to chief checker in the cursor department.

Despite the effort that Gumma and her dedicated crew put into making the hairlines in the cursors fine and straight, the slide rule remained an imprecise device. For discovering the final digits of an answer, the user had to rely on interpolation, on imagination. It was this quality of the slide rule—its bringing the user not to an absolute, indisputable answer, but only within the realm where the answer could be more or less accurately imagined—that won Gumma's affection, that made working with the rule as intriguing a pastime as reading detective stories. What Gumma understood at once—and she was always just a bit annoyed by the fact that she couldn't get anyone else to regard this fact with quite the awestruck reverence that she did—was that the hairline in the cursor did not reveal the answer to a problem: it concealed it. The edges of the hairline defined the limits of the range within which the answer lay; therefore the answer itself was under the hairline somewhere.

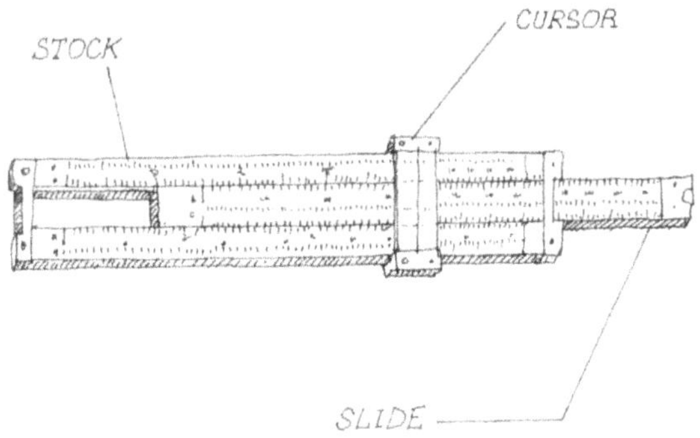

Gumma reserved for herself the best of the cursors that were produced there in the cursor room, the ones with the smoothest action, the ones with the finest and straightest hairlines. Each member of her crew would bring her any that seemed especially good pieces of work. If Gumma accepted one of these for her own, her having accepted it was a greater reward than the thanks she gave for it. But when she sat curled up on her sofa in the evening, working at recreational mathematics problems, even when she bent over the largest and finest rule in her collection, with a jeweler's loupe in her eye, she was only working at the edges of accuracy, she was only making tiny steps toward a more correct answer, the way the toast in her toaster made tiny steps from breadness to toastness.

7

SO THERE WE WERE, Gumma and Guppa and I, sitting in their living room after dinner on New Year's Day. Guppa had a fire going, and he was sitting in his comfortable chair doing his pigeonholes. Gumma was curled up on the sofa, working with her slide rule. I was on the floor in front of the fire, with a stack of birth announcements from recent issues of the *Babbington Reporter* and a stack of clean white cards. The room was cozy and quiet, with just the crackle of the fire, the flutter of Guppa's cards, the swish of the slide moving through the stock of Gumma's slide rule.

"Is it okay if we listen to the radio?" I asked.

"Of course, Peter," said Guppa. "I'll tune it in for you."

"Oh, don't get up, Guppa," I said. "I can tune it in by myself. Eliza showed me how to work it last night."

I went over to the radio and turned it on.

"This is a wonderful radio," I said. Neither Guppa nor Gumma said anything. "Gumma, you sure are lucky to have a wonderful radio like this," I said.

"Mmmm," said Gumma.

She bent over her slide rule and made some notations on a piece of paper. I switched to one of the international bands, and the room filled with a foreign howl. I twiddled the dial.

"Boy, it would be great to have a radio like this at home," I said.

The flutter of Guppa's cards.

"It wouldn't have to be as fancy as this," I said. "After all, I've already got a radio that gets the regular stations."

"Mmm-hmm," said Guppa. He knit his brows and bit his lower lip while he puzzled over one of the cards.

"What I need is a shortwave radio!" I said, as if the idea had just popped into my head from the ether. "If I had a shortwave radio, I'd be able to listen in on people's conversations from all over the place. I'd hear the rabble speaking in tongues. I might even pick up a few useful phrases."

"Yes, that's true," said Gumma, but I could tell that she was responding only to my tone of voice and that she hadn't really heard anything I'd said.

"I'll bet you could build a shortwave radio, couldn't you, Guppa," I said, loudly and proudly, very nearly shouting in his ear.

"What?" he asked, startled, looking up from his cards at last.

"You could build a shortwave radio, couldn't you?" I repeated.

"Well—" he began, and Gumma responded to *his* tone of voice as surely as she had responded to mine. She caught in the way he said "Well—" what might be the first note in a crescendo of self-deception that would end with his being committed to something long and complicated.

To tell the truth, I caught it too, and my heart beat a little faster and a smile came onto my face. I threw my arms around Guppa. "Oh, thanks, Guppa," I said. "This is going to be great fun!"

"Peter," said Gumma. "I'm not sure that your grandfather has the time to build a radio for you."

"Now Lorna," said Guppa, tousling my hair.

"Oh, Herb," said Gumma. She was smiling when she said it, and so was Guppa, and so was I.

8

WE WENT THROUGH back issues of *Impractical Craftsman* that evening, that first evening of the New Year. We found plans for many radios that might be suitable, but then Guppa came upon the one that was just right. The article began: "Here's a project that offers hour after interminable hour of baffling precision work, one that's sure to bring you an almost enervating sense of satisfaction when you've finally finished, one that is guaranteed to make your loved ones admire your stick-to-itiveness, your determination to see a difficult job through, your conviction that there is a right way of doing things, your unwillingness to cut corners."

"This sounds like the one for us," Guppa said.

9

OUR FIRST WORKING DAY was a Saturday. My father had driven me to Gumma and Guppa's on Friday night. I passed the night in restless impatience, eager for the work to begin, eager to be sitting beside Guppa in the cellar, to be working with him. I woke several times in the night, and was disappointed each time to find that the sun hadn't risen yet, to hear Guppa still snoring in the next room. Finally, enough gray light spread through the room so that when I climbed out of bed and stood close to the wall I could make out the branches and cherry blossoms on the wallpaper. I decided that morning had arrived and that things should get under way, so I dressed quickly and went to the kitchen to make some toast.

Gumma and Guppa loved to sleep late on weekends. When I was at home and wanted to talk to them on the telephone, I would have to wait until noon before I could call them. When I was spending a weekend with them, I knew that I had to be quiet until they were up, but there was always something interesting to look forward to on those weekends, something that made me impatient and restless, something that made me get up early. Gumma and I might be going to plant bulbs or bake bread or fry doughnuts. Guppa and I might be going to build a submarine out of oil drums or buy a Geiger counter and see if we could find any uranium deposits in the back yard or spread a new batch of clamshells on the driveway or just drive around town in the Studebaker looking to see if anybody had thrown away anything interesting. I would always be in a hurry to get going on these projects, so I would wake early. I would get up on my own and wander around the house for hours until Gumma and Guppa woke up.

I filled these morning hours by playing with their cat, by drawing pictures at Guppa's desk, and—when I was old enough—by making toast.

This morning, I had already played with the cat. I had even fed him, given him fresh water, and let him in and out of the house several times. I had drawn several pictures, each of which was a landscape that featured a pond (because I had just learned to draw ponds with pretty convincing perspective and particularly enjoyed complicating their shorelines with points and lagoons), clouds (because I had also just learned to draw nice, plump, billowy cumulus clouds), shadows (because I got a kick out of using the side of the pencil point to shade things), a disproportionately large duck (because Guppa had a nice little cast-metal Merganser paperweight that I wanted very much to learn to draw), and the transparent moon that sometimes graces the daytime sky (because I had begun to develop a fondness for it that still persists). I had made myself three slices of toast and eaten one with butter, one with butter and peanut butter, and one with butter and strawberry jam.

I was lying on the living-room rug in the light that fell through the windows in the front door. There were four diamond-shaped windows, themselves arranged in a diamond. The door was black and massive, made of wood, with iron strap hinges that ran nearly its entire width. It was rounded at the top. January sunlight fell in shafts through the windows, and in the shafts of sunlight, dust was dancing.

Why, I wondered, *does the dust dance that way?*

After some experimentation, I thought that I had found the answer. The dust was alive. (I did not believe this, of course; I was merely passing the time until Gumma and Guppa got up.) From the conclusion that the dust dancing in the air was alive, it was not a great leap to the idea that the dust on the floor must be dead. There wasn't a lot of dust on the floor; just enough. I picked up a little on my finger and blew it into the sunlight. It leaped and danced with more vigor than the dust I had been watching. I had been wrong! The dust on the floor was just resting, sleeping late, like Gumma and Guppa.

(My morning wasn't being wasted: I was exercising the faculty of human reasoning. I had accumulated some information and I had detected in it or pretended to detect in it certain patterns, and from them I had drawn a couple of conclusions. Then, as happens as often as not, along came some new information, and I was forced to recognize that the conclusion was wrong or not quite right. I took the old information and the new information, shook them well together, and poured out a new conclusion. I had to do quite a lot of this while I was growing up, and I found, frequently, that my conclusions made adults—and even older children—laugh, so when a private opportunity to practice arose—as this one had—I seized it. However, the affection that I had developed for any of my old conclusions was likely to persist strongly enough to leave its mark on a new one, and over the course of time I've found that I grow fonder and fonder of certain of the *old* conclusions and wearier and wearier of accommodating new information.)

I had decided that the dust on the floor wasn't dead; it was just resting. Perhaps I was on to something. I'd have to gather more information. I went down to the cellar, where there was plenty of dust. I ran a series of tests. A lot of the dust down there turned out to be just resting too, even the sawdust. I sat down and thought. The idea came to me that everything, everything I saw and touched, even the air I moved through, was moving, was in a sense alive.

"Peter, are you down there?" It was Gumma, calling me from the top of the cellar stairs.

"Yes, Gumma," I called. "I was just—"

I hesitated. Was I going to say that I was just looking at dust? I had enough experience with adults to know that that probably wouldn't be well received.

"— waiting for Guppa," I said.

"You have to be patient, Peter," said Gumma. "You have to remember that Guppa works very hard all week long, and he needs his rest on the weekends. It's the only time he has to sleep late."

I'd gotten myself into a mess. "Oh, I know that," I said. "That's why I was being so quiet, and I was sweeping up dust in the cellar to help him out."

"You're a good boy, Peter," said Gumma, in a voice as warm as a hug. "Come on up and help me make breakfast." She knew that this was a reward, since I liked helping her with any kitchen work, though I especially enjoyed using the toaster.

The smell of coffee and bacon drew Guppa out of bed soon enough, and he arrived in the kitchen as bright-eyed and eager to begin work as I had been when I awoke, hours before.

"Well, Peter," he said. "Up 'n' at 'em 'n' eager to go, are you?"

Some of my enthusiasm had worn off while I waited. I had made the mistake of imagining what work we would do, imagining my excitement, imagining the parts in my hands, Guppa's voice reading slowly through the instructions, and I had become a bit bored by the day's work. I was, after all, going to have to go through it for a second time.

"Yessiree!" I said, but my eagerness was forced, and it gave to the whole undertaking, before it had even really begun, the insidious suggestion of error, of something wrong enough at the start that it can't be put right by the end. If this feeling were an odor, it would smell like wet wool.

10

"FIRST we have to read the directions carefully," said Guppa. "Before you begin any project like this, you've got to read the directions a few times, until you know them pretty well. Then you can start to work, but you don't just jump right in and start doing the first thing. Understand?"

"Oh, yeah, I understand," I said, wanting for all the world to jump right in and start doing the first thing, whatever that might be. I pulled my metal stool up to Guppa's workbench, moving in as close to him as I could. Here we were, working on a project together, and we were going to do everything just right, just the way it should be done. First, we'd read the directions carefully, several times.

Guppa bent over the old issue of *Impractical Craftsman*. He moved his finger along as he read the directions, and now and then he commented to himself under his breath.

"Ah-ha!" he might say

Or, "Hmmph!"

Or, "Well, well, well."

Sometimes he would underline something with a flat red carpenter's pencil.

I read along too, and now and then, to make certain that everything was done right, I commented to myself under my breath. Sometimes I asked Guppa a question.

"What's this mean—*superheterodyne*?" I asked, pointing to the word in the second paragraph, where it had stopped me cold.

"Ah-ha!" said Guppa, and he underlined the word with his pencil. "That's what kind of radio it will be, when we're finished," he said.

"What about *triode*?" I asked a little later.

"That's got something to do with it too," Guppa said, "but it's not really as important." A moment passed. "Well, come to think of it, it might be pretty important at that," he said. He went back and underlined it. He read on. I tried to keep up with him, but I ran into so many words that I didn't know that I gave up trying to read and put my effort into daydreaming about the real work of building the radio, the work that would begin after we had read the directions a few more times, and into saying "Ah-ha!" and "Gosh!" and "Hmmmm" under my breath.

When Guppa had finished reading the directions, he began reading them again, and I began turning on my stool and looking around the cellar. When he had finished reading the directions a second time, he began reading them *again,* and I began fooling around with the wringer on Gumma's washing machine. When he had finished reading the directions for the third time, he straightened up and rubbed his back and then flipped back to the start again.

"You hungry, Guppa?" I asked. He turned to me with a look of some surprise, as if he had forgotten that I was there.

"Hungry?" he asked. "No, not yet, Peter."

"When do you think you'll want lunch?" I asked.

He looked at me and smiled. "Oh, in a little while, I guess," he said.

"Maybe I should go upstairs and help Gumma make some sandwiches," I suggested.

He looked at me for a minute before he said anything. "Maybe you should," he said at last.

Gumma and I worked together on lunch. We made Guppa's favorite, raw onion sandwiches, on toast, with butter. Gumma sliced the onions, as she always did, and she was a marvel to watch. With her old knife, worn by sharpening so that the blade arched upward, she cut uniform slices, with the precision of one of the women in the ruling room at the slide-rule factory. I got to make the toast, and spread butter on it, and lay the slices of raw onion on it, and I carried a tray with two glasses of milk and a plate of the sandwiches to the cellar. They were delicious.

11

GUPPA DROVE HIS STUDEBAKER slowly along the highway, watching for Two Regular Joes Electrical

Gadgets, the store where we would buy the parts for the radio. We were more than half an hour west of Babbington, in an area where I had never been before. The road was crowded with cars. Now and then a driver would pull out from behind us and rush past honking his horn and shaking his fist, but Guppa ignored all of them, and I tried to ignore them too. My heart beat quickly with the excitement of this adventure, of being in unfamiliar territory, on an unfamiliar errand.

"There it is, Guppa!" I cried. It was a large cement-block building, painted yellow. The name was painted in enormous black letters along the side and repeated in a huge neon sign on the roof and again in metal letters above the front windows.

Guppa pulled off the road and parked in front of the building. When I got out of the car, my knees were weak with excitement.

Hand-painted across the door was the motto, "If we don't got it, you don't need it," and as soon as we entered the store, I knew that it was so. The place was entirely filled with things that I had never seen before. Most of what was for sale there did not even resemble anything that I had seen before. Not only was everything unfamiliar, but none of it gave, from outward appearance, any hint of what it was supposed to do or how it might be used. Among stores, Two Regular Joes Electrical Gadgets immediately leaped to the foremost spot in my affection, dropping the Babbington Army-Navy Surplus Store to second and Arnberg's Hardware and Sick-room Supply to a distant third. The mystery, the subtlety of these gadgets won me immediately; a nail and a hammer give themselves away at once, but a soldering iron and a capacitor do not. I stood inside the door for a few breaths, just looking around, and I think my mouth was hanging open. I know that when I looked at Guppa *his* mouth was hanging open.

Guppa opened his *Impractical Craftsman* to the list of materials for the receiving set. He looked at the list for a while, muttering to himself, and then he looked up and down the rows of shelves.

Directly in front of us were some gadgets made of black-painted metal, roughly rectangular, with an open section in the middle filled with a cylinder that seemed to be made of brown paper. Shiny, coppery wires projected from the bottom of the paper cylinder. These things came in several sizes, and they had a nice heft to them. The paper part was coated with or soaked in wax, and so felt soft and sticky. I hoped that we'd need a few of these.

"Do we need any of these, Guppa?" I asked.

"Hmmm, let's see," he said. He stared at the list for a while. "No, I guess we can do without those," he said.

"How about just one?" I asked.

"Peter," said Guppa, "why don't you just look around for a while? I'm going to have that clerk help me find some of the things we need. That'll save some time."

"Okay, Guppa," I said.

Guppa walked over to a counter where a thin, dark-haired man, probably one of the two regular Joes, was reading a newspaper.

"Morning," said Guppa.

The man looked up. "Do something for you?" he asked.

"My grandson and I are going to build a shortwave receiving set," said Guppa.

"Great," said the man. He began chewing on his thumbnail.

"We're going to need some parts," said Guppa. "Wire, for instance, and, well, that sort of thing."

The clerk raised an eyebrow and smiled with only the left side of his mouth. I tried doing it myself. "You got a list?" he asked.

"Right here," said Guppa, and he released lots of air with the words. He opened the magazine on the counter.

The clerk looked at the list and said almost at once, "Sure, we've got all of this stuff."

"I want only the best," said Guppa, in a louder voice. "And all new. I don't want any rebuilt triodes or any of that."

The clerk laughed and shook his head. Guppa knitted his brows for a moment and stared hard at the clerk. Then he relaxed and laughed too.

"Heh-heh-heh," he laughed.

"Heh-heh-heh," the clerk laughed right back.

I began examining with minute care some mud-brown cylinders with wires sticking out of each end and bright painted bands of red, yellow, and orange along their sides.

12

I DRAGGED the metal stool up to the workbench and climbed onto it. I did not know then, and could not have known then, how much time I would spend on that stool in that cellar.

Guppa rubbed his hands together and reached for one of the several brown paper bags that he had brought home from the electrical gadget store. "Well, here we go," he said. He began pulling strange and wonderful objects from the bags and arranging them in a neat array on his workbench.

A few things have reappeared at intervals throughout my life, like motifs, like variations on a little phrase in a sonata. Among these are clams, of course, and a particularly unattractive plaid that first appeared on a bathing suit my mother bought me during the fat period of my childhood, and workbenches. I've always taken great pleasure in seeing anyone's workbench, for a workbench is, I think, a window on one's aesthetic soul. To be permitted to see a person's workbench is, for me, a sign of great intimacy, particularly if the workbench is in the cellar, because merely to be invited to the cellar is a token of close affection.

Guppa's workbench was small and old. It was certainly less than half the size of Big Grandfather's workbench. Both grandfathers kept neat, orderly workbenches, but Guppa's style of neatness and organization differed from Big Grandfather's. It was a case of a difference in degree producing a clear difference in style. Along shallow shelves above Big Grandfather's workbench stood rows of identical jelly jars, each labeled to describe its contents, and each containing only items that were quite precisely alike. Big Grandfather's level of categorization was highly refined. One jar, for example, contained only brass screws one inch long; another contained only blue steel tacks one-half inch long. Any item that Grandfather did not feel comfortable putting into an existing jar had to have a new jar of its own. As a result, many of the jars held a single item.

Guppa, on the other hand, kept his supplies in large cans and large categories, such as "screws," "springs," and "string." Whenever he needed a brass screw one inch long, he would dump all the screws out onto his bench and poke through them for a pleasant interval, whistling with the carefree pleasure of this simple task, until he found the screw he needed.

The screw supplies of both grandfathers also offered vivid evidence of the strongest of the many attitudes that they had in common: frugality. Each grandfather had a great many screws that had been removed from household objects in the course of repair work or, if the objects were beyond repair, removed as part of a stripping operation before they were thrown out. The screws had been removed at the expense of no small labor, yet most of these salvaged screws were unusable. Their slots were so worn or filled with paint that driving one of them into a hole would require great effort and concentration and an incredibly high tolerance for frustration. These qualities both grandfathers possessed in abundance. I do not. If I encounter difficulty in driving a screw into a wall to hold a shelf, for example, I am likely to abandon the project, or drive the screw in with a few vicious blows from a heavy hammer, or tear the half-hung shelf off the wall and throw it through a window. And yet, in my cellar there are jars chock full of screws that are entirely unusable. Whatever it was that made it so hard for my grandfathers to throw a screw away they passed along to me.

My father's workbench was quite a different matter. It was so cluttered with tools and scraps that no work surface was exposed anymore. Since the workbench had become storage space, any work on a project had to be performed on the cellar floor or on a couple of planks thrown over a couple of sawhorses. If you had seen my father's workbench, you might have thought that its clutter was a sign of a sloppy mind, but it was not at all; it was merely an expression of a workbench aesthetic different from my grandfathers'. My father knew more or less precisely where everything on the workbench was; he could, for example, reach behind him while he was measuring a board and grab a carpenter's pencil with very little groping, and of the several cords that were entwined among the clutter, he could most of the time pick out the one that belonged to the tool he wanted and follow it from the plug on up to the tool itself.

The two aesthetics—neatness and clutter—are at war within me, and from the state of my workbench one can tell at any time which has, temporarily, the upper hand. I was surprised and delighted to find, when Albertine and I first thought of buying the place, that Small's Hotel had a fine, large, solid workbench. Things have a way of accumulating on this bench until the clutter resembles that on my father's workbench, though it never quite comes up to that standard. When it reaches a certain level of clutter, a level that I can recognize quite precisely even though the contents of the clutter are never the same, I swing in the direction of my grandfathers and spend a day or two putting things in their proper places and putting old screws and nails into jars and plastic containers. Al is always delighted to see the grandfathers beginning to get the upper hand again, and while I bustle around in the cellar it is not unusual to hear her playing something sprightly on the piano in the ballroom just above me.

As Guppa removed the wonderful gadgets from the paper bags, he arranged them in ranks by type, and I helped out by arranging them within the ranks by size.

13

FROM ONE OF THE BAGS Guppa pulled a couple of the hefty rectangular objects that I had admired at the store.

"Oh, great," I said. "You got some of those." I held one in either hand and enjoyed the weight of them. "Thanks, Guppa," I said, and I gave him a hug. "It's going to look a lot more solid with a couple of these on it."

Guppa chuckled and patted me on the head.

"What should I do?" I asked.

"Well," said Guppa, "we have to make a chassis out of this sheet metal."

Make a chassis out of sheet metal! Wow! I had no idea what a chassis was, but I could see that the sheet metal was, by its very nature—its precise rectangularity, its hardness, its smoothness, the whoomp-whoomp sound it made when I flexed it in my hands—going to be lots of fun to work with.

"I'll get started on that," I said. "What do I do?"

Guppa looked at me and tightened his lips. When he spoke, he used the soft voice that he used when he told me that it was time for bed. "Well, Peter, we have some things to do that you don't know how to do yet. You'll just have to be patient for a while and watch me. After I show you how to do things, you can try them, okay?"

"Sure!" I said. It seemed like a fair enough deal to me. I wanted to work on the radio, of course, but I didn't want the results marred by the sloppy sort of work that an untrained kid like me would produce.

Guppa began fabricating the chassis. It turned out to be even more fun than I had imagined. It involved lots of sawing with a hacksaw that went *scree-scree* through the metal, sending thrilling chills up and down our spines, plenty of whanging and banging at the metal while it was clamped in a vise, a good deal of drilling with Guppa's hefty electric drill, which squealed through the metal and threw bright, sharp-edged helixes all over the workbench and onto the floor, and quite a bit of cursing, mostly under the breath, but occasionally loud enough to bring Gumma to the cellar door to call out, "Are you sure you know what you're doing, Herb?"

It also involved some sweeping up, and that's what I did.

14

I WILL NOT make you sit through each step in the building of the radio. We began, you will recall, in January. By the time the crocuses began to pop up in corners of Gumma and Guppa's lawn, the chassis looked quite complete from the top. There were handsome black sockets that would hold the tubes and coils, and there were stocky transformers and some shiny things that looked like little cans. On the front of the chassis were six knobs in a row and a shiny toggle switch that would, one day, make the tubes light up and send unfamiliar sounds into the earphones. Looking underneath, one got an idea of how far we still had to go. Each of the gadgets mounted on top bristled with prongs and lugs underneath, and even I could figure out that all of those had to be connected with some of the wire that Guppa had bought. There were still lots of gadgets, most of them pretty small, lined up on the workbench, and I supposed that all of them had to go in there somewhere. I had developed a deep admiration for Guppa's stick-to-itiveness that persists to this day. We had made two more excursions to the electrical gadget store to find out what some of the things lined up on the bench were and to replace tubes that had rolled onto the cellar floor. I had assumed for myself the job of sweeping the cellar while Guppa worked, and there was by this time so little dust left that I had to get down on my hands and knees and work at the floor with a whisk broom to fill the dustpan. I had taken to wearing the earphones while I worked and imagining the strange and wonderful things I would hear through them when the radio was ready.

By the time the first tomatoes ripened in Guppa's garden, the underside of the chassis looked like my father's workbench. Wires of many colors connected most of the prongs and lugs, and most of the colorful resistors and drab capacitors were hooked in there somehow too. Gumma had taught me how to bake bread, and I had become nearly as precise as she at slicing onions for onion sandwiches. I had swept dust from the walls around the cellar, and then, with no more dust available, had given up sweeping the cellar, and had sat on the metal stool beside Guppa, watching him solder connection after connection.

When Thanksgiving arrived, Gumma taught me to make chestnut stuffing, and Guppa and I believed that we had the radio licked. Everything was in place, except for a few extra resistors and capacitors, but on another trip to the gadget store one of the Regular Joes assured Guppa that these leftovers had been included in the parts list only as spares. Guppa brought the radio up from the cellar after Thanksgiving dinner and plunked it down in the middle of the table, where it occasioned as much oohing and ahing as the turkey had. Well, perhaps not as much as the turkey, but at least as much as the Waldorf salad. Guppa beamed. He pushed his chair back from the table and took a cigarette from my father's pack. He gave an account of the labor that had been involved so far, and I could see that everyone admired his stick-to-itiveness.

"All we have to do now," he said, "is wind the coils."

15

THEN CAME THE FLOOD. Gumma and Guppa lived near Bolotomy Bay, about half a foot above sea level. Every fall, during the hurricane season, high tides during storms would send a couple of inches of bay water into Gumma and Guppa's cellar. This year had been without hurricanes during the usual season, but a whopper of a storm struck during the weekend after Thanksgiving.

When I got up that Saturday, the whole world was howling and whining. The house felt cold, the cat wouldn't come out from under the living room sofa, and the toaster wouldn't work. I had taken to inspecting the radio alone in the mornings before Guppa woke up. I opened the door to the cellar and started down the stairs. When I got two-thirds of the way down, I was up to my knees in water.

Anything buoyant bobbed lethargically on the surface of the water, including, here and there, the vacuum tubes that were supposed to go into the radio. I knew that I was up to my knees in a disaster. My first thought was that the radio was doomed. It would never be completed now. Disappointment mingled with an odd sense of release. There was a lump in my throat, but my mouth was twisted into a strange smile, not unlike the one that I had seen the Regular Joes use on our visits to their store.

When Guppa saw the damage, he sprang into action at once. He had, years ago, built a powerful pump from parts of a cement mixer and an outboard motor, for just such an occasion. He improvised a ramp and wheeled the pump into the kitchen. By the afternoon he had pumped the cellar dry, flooded No Bridge Road, and filled the kitchen with oily soot.

Gumma and I worked at cleaning the kitchen, while Guppa rigged up the fans that he had built for drying out the waterlogged contents of the cellar. ("Surplus Wind Machine Makes Neat Rig for Drying Waterlogged Cellar Contents," *Impractical Craftsman,* Volume XVIII, Number 3, pages 48–52.)

By the following weekend, Guppa was back at work on the radio, and I was sitting on the metal stool watching him. He began winding the coils.

16

ON CHRISTMAS EVE, Guppa was bent over his workbench, winding loop after loop of fine varnished wire around a core of purple Bakelite, straining his eyes and his patience. He worked slowly and carefully, and as he worked he counted the windings, muttering the count to himself, repeating and repeating each number so that he wouldn't lose it in the foggy tedium of the winding. I was doing all that I could to help him: first, I was being very quiet, trying as hard as I could not to create any distraction that would make him lose track of what he was doing, nothing that would make him lose count of the windings on the coil; second, I was trying, by smiling a lot and holding my eyes wide, to show how delighted and amazed I was by the work that he was doing, how impressed I was by his stick-to-itiveness.

It was almost time for dinner. In the morning, right after an early breakfast, much earlier than Guppa was accustomed to on a day that was not a workday, seven hours and twenty-two minutes ago, we had come down to the cellar, and Guppa had begun trying to wind this, the final coil. Guppa had not even taken a break for lunch. I had tiptoed upstairs and made some onion sandwiches for us, on dark bread, bread that I had baked myself, and had brought the sandwiches and two glasses of milk to the cellar, stepping carefully down the stairs so that the scraping of my shoes wouldn't make Guppa lose count. Guppa's milk and sandwiches lay untouched on the plate. The bread had curled as it dried.

Guppa's work on the receiving set since January had, little by little, step by step—some steps forward and some steps backward and some off on dead-end side streets—transformed a couple of bags of electrical gadgets into something that was now very nearly a radio, but that would not cross the threshold to radio-ness until this last difficult coil was complete. Until it was successfully wound, all the effort throughout the year would only be effort expended in an *attempt* to build a radio; but with the completion of this coil, the effort would become effort expended in the *building* of a radio. I had stuck with Guppa throughout all the effort, all the time, that he had been at work on this, except for time that I spent upstairs making sandwiches or helping Gumma with other chores, and even that work was indirectly helpful, I like to think. My situation, waiting for Guppa to complete the almost magical transformation of these electrical gadgets, was a lot like that of a child who has put a slice of bread into a toaster and sits, still sleepy-eyed, waiting for the toaster to transform the bread to toast.

Most children do not have a good sense of the amount of work required to build a radio from scratch or of the amount of time required to do it or—for that matter—of the passage of time itself. For most of them, time is like a dotted line, with unequal sections of the line itself (events) and unequal interstices (non-events, the periods of waiting for something to happen that make up much of a person's childhood). I blame this misconception on the type of toaster used in most households: the pop-up toaster. In operating a pop-up toaster, one inserts a batch of bread (usually a slice or two) and lowers it into the toaster. For the child who watches this operation, the lowering of the bread is apparently the last event that occurs for some time, since the string of small events that add up to the toasting of the bread—the real work of toasting the bread—takes place out of the child's sight. Therefore, the toasting itself becomes one of those interstices between events, a nonevent, a period of waiting that varies, both in real and in apparent length, according to the hunger of the child, the thickness of the bread, and random fluctuations in the voltage of the electrical service to the toaster. When the toast pops up, the child at last witnesses another event, which terminates the period of waiting for something to happen.

What effect, we might ask ourselves, does the pop-up toaster have on the intellectual development of the child who sits beside it, morning after morning, waiting with his plate and peanut butter? Bread goes in as bread and comes out, after an interval, as toast. Put in bread. Wait. Get out toast. Surely, the child who watches this happen over a period of time comes to think of bread as *either* bread or toast, to think of time as discrete intervals, and to think of being as being in some one form or in some other, with intervals of waiting, intervals between states when, apparently, nothing happens. Such a child would ask his grandfather to build him a radio (that is, lower the bread into the toaster), wait for some interval, and then expect his grandfather to hand him a radio (that is, expect the toast to pop up). When they grow up, these children are immediately attracted to the quantum theory, digital watches, and electronic calculators.

I was not such a child, because Gumma and Guppa did not have a pop-up toaster. Their toaster was a chrome-plated metal box about as long as three slices of bread lined up side by side. At each end of the box was a slot a little higher than the height of a slice of bread and a little wider than the thickness of a slice of bread. Inside the box was a tunnel through which the toast moved from the left end of the toaster to the right. Along the bottom of the tunnel was a set of toothed rails linked by an armature to a motor. The motor made the rails raise the toast, move it a short distance to the right, and set it down again on the stationary base rail. On either side of the tunnel were resistance wires that provided the heat to toast the bread. Little by little, as the bread marched through the toaster, it browned; that is, it became toast.

Now here comes the best part. The manufacturer of this toaster, clearly nobody's fool, had provided a small circular window in the side, so that one could watch the rhythmic rightward shuffle of the slices of bread and their progress from bread to toast.

From a very early age, I loved watching—and listening to—the operation of this toaster. As the toaster operated, it produced a repetitive sound from somewhere inside the machine, from the scraping of some parts against others, a sound that I interpreted as words, the words *Annie ate her radiator,* repeated over and over while the bread toasted. I would sit and watch and listen to the toaster and watch the bread through the little window and try to decide where in its passage from left to right it became toast. And from that toaster I learned to think of time as a belt, to think of being as being in transit, and I laid the groundwork for a persistent nostalgic affection for the wave theory of electromagnetic radiation and round-faced watches and slide rules, and I developed a sense of time's passing.

During the forty-six weekends that I had so far spent with Guppa in the cellar working on the receiving set (not counting the time that we had spent pumping the cellar out and drying its contents after the flood in November), my sense of the passing of time had developed to a point where, although it may not have been as acute as my sense of sight, it was at least as sharp as my sense of smell.

When Guppa and I had begun work on the receiving set, we had, each in his mind's eye, pictured a similar tableau: grandfather and grandson bent to the work together, youth and age, experience and enthusiasm, harnessed in tandem. We had glowed for a while with the flush of a mutual overconfidence in what an enthusiastic grandson might be able to accomplish, guided by his grandfather's hand. That glow had faded pretty early in the course of the work, as soon as we had come to see that there was very little that I could do that Guppa would not have to undo or redo later. My helping had degenerated into my keeping out of Guppa's way and keeping him company, demonstrating by my presence, and by displays of enthusiasm, that I was grateful for the effort that he was making, that I was impressed as could be by his stick-to-itiveness, and that I was still crazy about the idea of having a shortwave receiving set, although in fact I had begun to think, halfway through our third day in the cellar, that I would have been a lot better off if I had asked Guppa to make me something quick and simple, like a scooter, just as I was sometimes struck by the thought, while watching a slice of white bread move through the toaster, that I would rather have had raisin bread.

17

LET ME EXPLAIN these coils that were giving Guppa so much trouble. The reason one radio can pick up signals that another cannot is that each of them is tuned to a different range of radio frequencies. The radio that Guppa was building for me would detect signals in the range of frequencies that are called "shortwave." Now within that broad range lie narrower "bands." The receiver would be able to receive signals in many of these bands, depending on which coil was plugged into its circuit. To change from one band to another, all I would have to do was unplug one coil and plug in another. The coils were to be wound on hollow Bakelite forms with pins projecting from their bases that could be inserted into sockets like those into which vacuum tubes were inserted.

When Guppa and I were looking through his back issues of *Impractical Craftsman* to decide what sort of radio we would build, we had found other, simpler radios, but Guppa had liked the notion of winding these coils by hand, and the thin, shiny wire had appealed to him as soon as he saw it in the electrical gadget store, but what had really persuaded him that this radio was just the one for us to build was the description of the work that appeared in the article: the hours of baffling precision work.

18

GUPPA HAD SPENT forty-six weekends in the cellar at work on the radio, discounting the time that he had spent pumping the cellar out and drying its contents. He had put eight hundred twenty-eight hours into the project. I had put in four hundred fourteen hours in the cellar and another seventy-eight making onion sandwiches and pouring coffee. I had made one hundred thirty-eight onion sandwiches, not counting the one that a boy from across No Bridge Road, a boy that I never knew by any other name but Frankie, left half-eaten on his plate when he came over one Saturday at noontime to see if I wanted to climb trees with him.

"There!" said Guppa at last. He turned toward me, raising the finished coil, the final coil, in a shaking hand. He had aged a great deal during the time that he had been at work on the radio. His eyes were red and teary, and the skin below them hung in dark, flaccid folds. His lips trembled and twitched with the effort to form a grandfatherly smile.

"That's great, Guppa!" I cried, with deep, genuine enthusiasm. The coil-winding was at last complete, the receiver was at last complete, a phase of my life had come to a crisp and clear conclusion. There was no ambiguity, no fuzzy line, no indeterminate point like that between breadness and toastness in Gumma's toaster, no need for interpolation. This moment marked the end of the work on the radio, and anything to follow, whatever it might be, would be a post-radio-construction event.

"This was the hardest one of all, wasn't it?" I asked. I knew that it had been; I had been able to see that it had been, even though I avoided watching Guppa too carefully and hoped that he did not know that I knew how many times he had unwound the coil and begun winding it again when he lost count of the windings.

"Well, yes, it was," he acknowledged.

I could see him gaining in strength now that the winding was done, now that everything was done. He was beginning to allow himself to feel proud.

"A job like this has got to be done just right," he said, raising the coil a little higher in a steadier hand. "If you're not ready to do what has to be done the way it should be done, then you're not ready to do it at all. Now, you take this coil. I could probably have been off by a few turns and it wouldn't have made all that much difference, except to me. I'd know that it wasn't right. That's why I had to stick to it until it *was* right."

Now he was glowing. His hand was firm, and he drew in deep breaths of the damp cellar air. He could relax now. He and I would be able to straighten things up on the bench, put the few remaining leftover parts into the electrical gadget jar, go upstairs to the kitchen, smiling so that Gumma would say that we looked like the cat that swallowed the canary, tell her about the progress we had made, then surprise her with the finished radio, listen to a few foreign broadcasts, show the radio to my parents when they arrived, eat dinner, sit in the living room and listen for a while longer, and then go to bed, content.

I heard the door at the top of the stairs open, and I heard rapid, brisk footsteps coming down the stairs. Mr. Beaker popped around the corner.

"What industry!" he cried. "You two haven't seen the light of day since breakfast, I understand."

He leaned back in an exaggerated pose and scrutinized us with exaggerated care.

"Hmmmm," he said. "From the fact that you got up so early, Herb, and from the little grins that you two are wearing, I'd say that you're getting very close to the end of this project. How's the work going?"

With pride, I announced to him that Guppa had wound all the coils and we would be listening in on the babble of foreign tongues any minute now.

"Take a look at this," I said. I picked up the coil that Guppa had finished. "This was the toughest one of all. It has the finest wire and the most windings."

"That is quite a piece of work," said Mr. Beaker. He took the coil from me and held it in front of him, raising it to eye level as if it were a jewel. "Quite a piece of work," he repeated. He looked closely at the coil and said, "Mm-mm-mm." He compressed his lips and nodded his approval. "How many windings does this have?" he asked Guppa.

Guppa had been smiling, standing with his hands in his pockets and rocking on his heels. Mr. Beaker's question had a visible effect on him, the same effect as a sudden increase in the mass of the earth would have had. All of Guppa seemed to slump.

"How many windings?" Guppa asked.

"Yes," said Mr. Beaker. "How many windings?"

My throat became dry, my palms moist. I knew that something was terribly wrong. I didn't want to look at Guppa, but I couldn't look away from him. He pulled his hands from his pockets and swept them through his hair, pushing it back from his forehead.

"It's got about—"

He looked at me. I gave him a jaunty smile that I intended to mean "I have every confidence in you, Guppa. You're my hero." He squinted his eyes and peered at me as if he had forgotten who I was.

"I don't know," he said. "It was in the hundreds—I know that." He turned toward the plans, open on his workbench, then turned away quickly, as if looking at the plans would have been cheating. "I'm sure I got it right," he said. He seemed to be pleading.

"Me too!" I said, with great verve and the conviction that came from a heartfelt desire not to have him wind the coil again.

"I'm sure that a few turns more or less won't make enough difference for anyone to notice anyway," said Mr. Beaker. He put the coil down on the bench.

Guppa picked the coil up and peered at it, as if by looking closely enough he would have been able to remember exactly how many turns of that fine varnished wire he had made. He sighed. "We'll try again tomorrow," he said. "What do you say we quit for the day and get something to eat?"

"Oh, yeah!" I cried. I dashed toward the stairs and pounded up them. I had to get away from Guppa. There was a lump in my throat, and I could feel the tears forming in my eyes. I felt horribly sorry for Guppa, who so wanted to please and impress me, and I felt sorry for myself, too, for I was now going to have to spend God knows how much longer sitting on the cold metal stool beside Guppa watching him rewind that damned coil.

19

BUT I DIDN'T HAVE TO, thanks to Gumma. When I told her what had happened, she got her slide rule and marched downstairs. She had Guppa and Mr. Beaker and me count and recount the number of windings we could see on the outside of the coil. She looked through the instructions and mumbled to herself. She measured the thickness of the windings on the coil and the thickness of the wire itself. Then she went to work with her slide rule. Guppa, Mr. Beaker, and I held our breath. If my heart hadn't been thumping so loudly,

I would have been able to hear the slide whispering through the stock.

Gumma took a deep breath. She smiled and let the breath out.

"It's exactly right," she said.

Mr. Beaker looked puzzled. "How many—" he began.

"Exactly right," Gumma repeated in a soft voice that reverberated through the cellar as if she had shouted.

"Yahoo!" I cheered.

Gumma gave Guppa a big hug, and so did I. Mr. Beaker gave him a pat on the back and said, "Well, you'll want to celebrate without me, so I'll head for home." No one said anything to him, so he left.

Gumma went back upstairs, and Guppa turned toward the workbench, but he was not close enough to it to read the instructions. I walked over to the workbench and closed the magazine.

"I'll help you straighten up, Guppa," I said, "and then we can go upstairs and try it out."

He didn't say anything. Hesitantly, I looked at him over my shoulder. He stood with his mouth in a rictus.

"I'll go put the magazine back," I said. "Why don't you clean the radio up with a rag so that it's nice and shiny when we take it upstairs?"

I walked upstairs with the magazine, and at the head of the stairs turned left, toward the back door, instead of right, toward the dining room, where Guppa had built the concealed bookcases that held his back issues of *Impractical Craftsman*. I went outside, onto the back porch, down the porch steps, and over to the trash cans. I lifted the lid of one and dropped the magazine in.

20

"CLOSE YOUR EYES, GUMMA," I said. "We're bringing it upstairs."

I opened the cellar door and peeked around it to make sure that Gumma had her eyes closed. She was holding her apron up over her eyes with both hands. The kitchen was full of the smell of turkey. I held the door open for Guppa, who was holding the radio in front of him in both hands. He set it on the kitchen table and plugged it in.

"Okay," I said, "you can look now." My skin was tingling all over with pride in Guppa, and with affection for the radio itself.

Gumma looked at the shining radio with wide eyes, and she began clucking and exclaiming over it. Guppa beamed, and so did I. At last, Guppa said, "What do you say we put it to the test?"

Gumma and I sat down at the table, silent and eager. Guppa switched the radio on. The tubes began to glow with tiny, intricate lines of orange light. Guppa put the earphones on and began twisting the dials. Gumma and I tried to read his expression. His smile slipped away, and he wrinkled his forehead and pursed his lips. He twisted the dials some more, and he tapped at a couple of the tubes. He wiggled the coil in its socket. Then he pulled the coil out and put in another.

"How is it, Guppa?" I asked. He looked at me, but I could tell from his expression that with the earphones on he hadn't made out what I had said.

"How is it?" I asked again, in a much louder voice. Guppa flashed a smile and nodded. Gumma put her arm across my shoulder. Guppa began twisting the dials and tapping the tubes again, and he began to frown. He pulled the second coil out and put in a third.

"Can I try?" I asked. I had to go to the bathroom, but I didn't want to leave the scene of all the excitement, so I was squeezing my legs together and bouncing up and down. Guppa didn't seem to hear me. Gumma tapped him on the shoulder, and he turned toward her with a start.

"What? What's the matter?" he asked in a loud voice.

"Peter wants to try listening," said Gumma, speaking with exaggerated precision.

Guppa looked at me, and he seemed terribly tired. My expression was beyond my control. I was smiling so completely that I couldn't speak when Guppa handed me the earphones. I slipped them on and fussed with them until they felt right or at least didn't hurt my ears too much. I cupped my hands over them and held them to my ears. The sound seemed to come at once from within me, from the earphones, and from someplace far away.

From a great distance came a sound like wind through willow trees, the rustle of the hanging branches of a weeping willow, the sweep of the branches along the ground. Winding through this was a deep and indecipherable murmur, like the voices of my parents and Gumma and Guppa when I had heard them talking together at night, years before, when I lay in my crib. And rising and falling through it all was a metallic sound, like the operation of a machine, very much like the scraping sound that Gumma's toaster made.

I looked at Guppa, who was looking at his shoes, and at Gumma, who was looking at me. Her lips were tight, and she was wringing her apron in her hands.

"It's just right, Guppa!" I said, and of course, with the earphones on and the static hissing in my ears I shouted it so loudly that Guppa looked up with a start and Gumma burst out laughing.

I twiddled the dials, and the rushing hiss faded and the murmur became a howl, the metallic scraping began to echo, and an irregular ticking began somewhere far away.

Gumma said, "Oh, Herb, I'm so proud of you," and Guppa shrugged and smiled. Gumma got up and poured

Guppa a glass of beer and then went back to making dinner, and Guppa went off to the living room. Neither of them asked to try the radio, and I didn't offer. When my parents arrived, I showed the radio to them but didn't let them listen to it, and then we ate dinner, and after dinner I insisted on taking it to bed with me.

21

GUPPA DIED when I was twenty-five, of a heart attack. Gumma died when I was twenty-eight, of cancer. I still have the radio. I keep it in the cellar, on an old maple table that was here when Al and I bought Small's Hotel. Beside the table is a wobbly straight-back chair. Sometimes, when I wake up in the middle of the night, I go to the cellar and put the earphones on, turn the set on, and sit and listen to the static. I know that, in a sense, the radio doesn't work, but I know too that in the night, sitting there alone in the cellar, dark except for the glow of the tubes, I can sometimes pick up, through the static, the flutter of Guppa's note cards, the whisper of Gumma's slide rule, the crackle of the living room fire, the scree-scree of Guppa's hacksaw, the Annie-ate-her-radiator-Annie-ate-her-radiator of the toaster, one of those sighs that Guppa let out while he worked on the coils, or the sound of my own footsteps scraping on the wooden stairs, when I came down to the cellar carrying a tray with two glasses of milk and a plate of onion sandwiches.

A NOTE TO THE READER

If you haven't read the preface to *The Static of the Spheres*, please read it now.

Thank you.

Peter Leroy

ABOUT THE AUTHOR

Peter Leroy spent his childhood and youth in the town of Babbington, New York, which lies on the South Shore of Long Island, between Nassau and Suffolk counties. As a teenager, he acquired considerable local fame as the "Birdboy of Babbington" after building a single-seat airplane in his family's garage and flying it to New Mexico and back, an achievement that in later life he admitted had become considerably exaggerated in the telling. Leroy and his wife, Albertine Gaudet, for many years ran Small's Hotel, on Small's Island, in Bolotomy Bay, off Babbington. His extensive, ongoing memoirs, *The Personal History, Adventures, Experiences & Observations of Peter Leroy,* are thoroughly flavored with the voice and style of Leroy himself—a self-described "muddleheaded dreamer," a rewriter of history, a man obsessed with the past as it was and as it might have been, the sly creator of his own salutary myth.

ABOUT THE AUTHOR

Eric Kraft grew up in Babylon, New York, on the South Shore of Long Island, where he was for a time co-owner and co-captain of a clam boat, which sank. He met or invented the character Peter Leroy while dozing over a German lesson during his first year at Harvard. The following year, he married his muse, Madeline Canning; they have two sons. After earning a Master's Degree from the Harvard Graduate School of Education, Kraft taught school in the Boston area for a while, moonlighting as a rock music critic for the *Boston Phoenix*. Since then, he has undertaken a variety of hackwork to support the Kraft ménage and the writing of the voluminous work of fiction that he calls *The Personal History, Adventures, Experiences & Observations of Peter Leroy*. He has been the recipient of a fellowship from the National Endowment for the Arts; was, briefly, chairman of PEN New England; and has been awarded the John Dos Passos Prize for Literature.

www.ingramcontent.com/pod-product-compliance
Ingram Content Group UK Ltd.
Pitfield, Milton Keynes, MK11 3LW, UK
UKHW020218250726
13967UKWH00001B/69

9 781105 747373